“要坚信，哪怕只有你自己。”

“Believe. Even if you're the only one.”

在 4000 米高的悬崖下面，有一座世外之城。

城里到处都是烟囱。

烟囱冒着黑烟，城市的上空烟雾蒙蒙。

从早到晚，一直烟雾蒙蒙。

城里的人们被困在黑烟中，没有人知道蓝色的天空，

没有人知道闪闪的星星。

There was a town isolated from the outside world, surrounded by a 4,000 meter tall cliff.

The town was full of chimneys.

Smoke rose from everywhere, clouding the sky above.

Smoke, smoke, from morning till night.

The people living in the chimney town were encaged in black smoke,

and did not know about the blue sky.

They did not know about the shining stars.

这一天是万圣节，烟囱之城沉浸在节日气氛中。

城中燃起篝火，烟雾弥漫，天空比往常更加灰蒙蒙了。

一名快递员匆忙穿行在浓烟滚滚的夜色中。

他一边走一边咳嗽，不小心把运送中的一颗心脏弄丢了。

周围什么都看不清，那颗心脏不知道落到哪里去了。

快递员只好放弃寻找，跑进浓雾里，消失在黑暗之中。

咚咚、咚咚、咚咚……

烟囱之城的一个角落里，那颗心脏正在跳动着。

The town was in the midst of the Halloween festival.

Joined by the smoke for warding off evil spirits, the town was even smokier than usual.

One day,

A deliveryman dashing across the night sky choked on the smoke

and carelessly dropped a heart he was delivering.

With such terrible visibility, there was no way to know where it fell.

The deliveryman quickly gave up and ran off into the night.

Thump thump, thump thump, thumpity thump thump.

The heart was beating in one corner of the chimney town.

烟囱之城

POUPELLE OF CHIMNEY TOWN

[日] 西野亮广 著　王志庚 译

新星出版社 NEW STAR PRESS

心脏落在了城外的一座垃圾山上。

咚咚跳个不停的心脏，沾满垃圾，变成了一个垃圾人。

垃圾人头戴破伞，口吐浊气，又脏又臭。

他侧耳倾听，远处传来一阵钟声。

除了他，这里好像还有别人。

垃圾人走出了垃圾山。

The heart fell on a pile of trash at the edge of town.
All types of rubbish stuck onto the thumping, beating heart, until finally a trashman was born.
His head was a shaggy old umbrella. Gas hissed out of his mouth.
He was a very filthy trashman. A very smelly trashman.
When he strained his ears, he could hear the sound of bells from the distance.
There seemed to be others.
The trashman left the trash pile.

垃圾人来到城里，看到很多怪物正在游行。

“喂，你装扮的是什么呀？”

垃圾人回头一看，只见一个南瓜怪站在面前。

“你是谁？”

“吞噬地狱之火，照亮万圣之夜。我是大名鼎鼎的杰克南瓜灯！”

When he arrived in town, it was full of monsters.
“Hey, you're dressed quite oddly.”
He turned around, where there stood a pumpkin monster.
“Who are you?”
“I swallow the flames of hell and illuminate the Halloween night with shady light.
I am Jack-o'-lantern!”

怪物们向垃圾人围拢过来。

“咦——嘿——嘿！我是恐怖之夜的主宰者，让所有人害怕的魔女！”

“我是科学怪人弗兰肯！”

“我是不会死的僵尸！”

大家一起问垃圾人：“你是什么怪物？”

“我是垃圾人。”

怪物们笑了起来。

All kinds of monsters started gathering around the trashman.
“Tee hee hee, I'm a witch, the ruler of night, and everybody's fear.”
“A monster created by a devilish scientist ; I am Mr. Frankenstein.”
“I forgot how to die. I am Zombie.”
Everybody started to ask.
“And just what in the world are you?”
“I'm a trashman.”
All the monsters burst out laughing.

ぬくもり工房
やすよ
寺田たけのこ店

垃圾人也加入怪物们的游行队伍，高喊着：

“不给糖就捣乱，不给糖就捣乱！”

他们挨家挨户去要糖果，

还给沿途的小孩子们送气球，

看着垃圾人吹的气球高高飘在空中，孩子们都很开心。

“走喽，去下一家啦，垃圾人。”

The trashman joined the monsters and went around houses shouting
"Trick or treat, trick or treat. Give us some treats or we're gonna trick you!"
and collected treats from all the adults.
Then, they went around giving balloons to the smaller children.
The trashman's balloons were very floaty, which delighted all the children.
"OK, next house. Let's go, trashman."

怪物们挨家挨户敲门，口袋里很快就塞满了糖果。

钟楼上的钟敲响了，怪物们要回家了。

垃圾人对其中一个伙伴说：

“万圣节真好玩儿，明天我们还来过节吧！”

“你说什么?! 垃圾人，万圣节今天就要结束了啊！”

说着，怪物们一个接一个地摘下面具。

南瓜怪是个男孩，叫安东尼奥。

魔女怪是个女孩，叫丽贝卡。

原来，大家都是假扮的怪物。

The monsters went around everywhere and their pockets full of treats.
The bell of the clock tower rang, and everyone started preparing to go home.
The trashman spoke to one of them.
“Halloween is fun. Let’s do it again tomorrow.”
“What are you talking about, trashman. Halloween is only today.”
And with that all, the monsters began taking off their masks.
Little boy Antonio came out of the pumpkin,
and little girl Rebecca came out of the witch.
They were only dressed like monsters.

晩喜酒
居酒屋
三郎
さぶろう
大倉
商店
ネモト
情熱の

“怎么啦，快把衣服换下来吧，垃圾人。”

“对呀，脏兮兮的，你自己也不喜欢吧？”

说着，丽贝卡伸手去拽垃圾人头上的伞。

“疼、疼、疼……”

“What's the matter, take yours off, too, trashman.”

“Yeah, you don't like that dirty costume either, do you?”

Rebecca tried to pull off trashman's head.

“Ow!”

POST

“啊——”丽贝卡不由地惊叫了一声。

“这家伙不是装扮的！”男孩们赶紧躲开。

“滚开！怪物！”

“滚吧，垃圾人！滚到海里去！”

男孩们说着脏话。

“Aaaaaaaargh!”
Rebecca let out a huge scream.
“This guy’s not in a costume!”
The boys quickly moved away from the trashman.
“Go away, monster!”
“Get out of town, trashman! Drain down to the sea!”
The boys shouted dirty words one after the other.

绝味珍味妙味
天地料理

关于垃圾人的传言，很快传遍了全城。

“垃圾人来了！”

“城里真的有怪物！”

垃圾人想解释，可是根本没有人听，人们高喊着：

“滚远点，垃圾人！”

“别碰我，臭怪物！”

垃圾人坐在凳子上，发出一阵叹息。

这时，耳边传来一个声音：

“你就是传说中的垃圾人？听说你不是装扮的？”

Word of the trashman quickly spread across town.
“It's a trashman.”
“There's a monster in town.”
When the trashman tried to speak, all he got was
“Go away, trashman,” “You're gonna get your smell on me.”
The trashman sat on a bench, and hissed out a stinky sigh.
That was when it happened.
“So you're the trashman everyone is talking about. I heard that's not a costume?”

dig me out
USAG

垃圾人抬头一看，一个浑身沾满煤灰的男孩站在他面前。

男孩知道垃圾人不是装扮的，但他并没有逃跑。

“我叫卢比奇，是烟囱清洁工。你呢？”

“这，这个嘛……”

“你没有名字吗？那就取一个吧。

对啦，你是万圣节那天来到这儿的，就叫‘万圣节·普佩尔’吧。”

When he turned around, he saw a boy covered in soot from head to toe.

The boy didn't run away even when he found out what the trashman was.

"I'm Lubicchi, the chimney cleaner. And you are?"

". . . Ummm"

"If you don't have a name, you should give yourself one. Let's see . . .

because you showed up on Halloween, your name is Halloween Poupelle."

カチカチ
サイダー
株式会社
日本
デザイン

“万圣节·普佩尔，你在这里做什么呢？”

“没有人愿意理我。”

听到普佩尔这么说，卢比奇哈哈大笑。

“那当然啦，普佩尔，你又脏又臭，有谁愿意跟你玩儿呢。”

“还说我呢，你自己不也黑不溜秋的嘛。”

"Halloween Poupelle, what are you doing here?"
"Nobody will play with me."
"Ha ha ha!" Lubicchi laughed as Poupelle said this.
"Obviously, Poupelle. You're dirty, and quite smelly, too."
"How dare you say! You're all dirty and black, too, Lubicchi."

三宿
山咲バル
CIGARETTE

“我刚下班，浑身都是煤灰，当然脏兮兮的。”

“清扫烟囱不是大人的工作吗？”

“我没有爸爸，所以必须出来工作。

好了，不说这些了，你浑身臭烘烘，没人会喜欢你的。

不如你来我家院子里洗个澡吧。”

“啊？可以吗？”

“反正我也得洗干净才能进屋，你也一起洗洗吧。”

“卢比奇，你为什么不讨厌我？”

“或许因为你身上有股熟悉的味道吧。像是我扔掉的脏裤子的味道。”

“Well, I'm on my way home from work, so as you can see, I'm covered in soot.”

“Isn't chimney cleaning a job for grownups?”

“I don't have a dad, so I gotta work.

Besides, with a smell like that, no wonder they don't like you. Why don't you wash yourself in our yard.”

“What? That's OK?”

“I need to wash up before I get in the house anyway. You should do the same.”

“Why don't you avoid me, Lubicchi?”

“You smell kinda familiar. I wonder if my dirty pants are mixed in there.”

(株)
清水表具店
級建築士事務所
KOYAMA
BAR
STOP
出入口

卢比奇仔仔细细地帮普佩尔洗了个澡。

普佩尔变得干干净净的，臭味也没了。

“卢比奇，谢谢你！”

“嗯……你的嘴巴还有点臭，你呼一口气。”

普佩尔呼了一口气。

“啊，真臭，普佩尔，闻起来像瓦斯一样，刷牙也没有用呢。”

他们俩一直玩儿到很晚。

Lubicchi washed every nook and cranny of Poupelle's body.

All the grime came cleanly off, and the smell was much better, too.

"Thank you, Lubicchi."

"Hmm . . . but your mouth is still stinky. Breathe out."

Poupelle exhaled out.

"Ha ha ha, that's so smelly. Poupelle, that's gas. Brushing is not gonna help."

The two played together till late that night.

太
郎
スナック
Roshan
石山ゴム
平林鉛筆
ひらばやしえんぴつ
Beauty
在間石鹸

“你今天和垃圾人一起玩儿了？”

“是的，妈妈。不过别担心，普佩尔不是坏人。”

“你的好奇心还真随你爸爸。”

卢比奇的爸爸是城里唯一的渔夫，去年冬天被海浪夺走了生命。

人们只找回来一条破烂的渔船。

烟囱之城的人们认为海里有妖怪，禁止出海打渔，

还说卢比奇的爸爸是“自作自受”。

“妈妈，你喜欢爸爸什么呢？”

“你爸爸很害羞，这一点还蛮可爱。他开心的时候，

总会用食指在鼻子下面蹭两下，就像这样。”

“Hey, did you play with that trashman today?”

“It's OK, Mom. Poupelle's not a bad guy.”

“You got that curiosity from your dad.”

Lubicchi's father was the only fisherman in town, but he was swallowed by the waves and died last winter.

The only thing they found was his fishing boat in tatters.

In this town, people believed that there were monsters in the ocean and it was forbidden to go out to sea ;

so the townsfolk said “He had it coming.”

“Say, Mom, what did you like about Dad?”

“He was shy and cute in a way, don't you think? When he was happy, he'd rub under his nose, like this.”

BEANS

第二天，普佩尔和卢比奇爬上了烟囱。

“我好害怕，卢比奇。”

“不用怕，抓紧一点就没事了。不过有时会刮起一阵风，小心别把东西掉下去啊。”

“你以前掉过什么东西吗？”

“嗯，一个镶着爸爸照片的银色吊坠。

我只有那一张爸爸的照片，可是，再也找不回来了。”

卢比奇指着下面的污水河说：“就掉在那条河里了。”

Next day, Poupelle and Lubicchi went up a chimney.

“I'm scared, Lubicchi.”

“You'll be fine, just hold on tightly. But it gets gusty, so be careful not to drop anything.”

“Have you dropped anything?”

“Yeah. A silver pendant with a picture of my dad.

That was the only picture of Dad I had. I looked, but couldn't find it.”

Lubicchi pointed at the sewage canal.

“It fell into that sewage canal.”

ひばり号
GO
KOH

“喂，普佩尔，你知道星星吗？”

“星星？”

“我们笼罩在烟雾里，所以看不到它们。

烟雾上空飘着很多闪闪发光的小石子，那就叫星星。

不是一颗两颗，而是千千万万颗，多得数都数不过来。”

“真的吗？你是在吹牛吧？”

“我爸爸见过星星。有一次他出海到了一个很远的地方，那里没有烟雾，

夜空中全都是一闪一闪的星星。不过，谁也不相信爸爸的话。

直到他死去，人们都认为他在撒谎，说他是骗子。

爸爸坚持说‘烟雾上面有星星’，还告诉我怎样才能看到星星。”

卢比奇抬头望着夜空中的烟雾说，

“‘要坚信，哪怕只有你自己。’”

"Say Poupelle, do you know what a '*star*' is?"

"A star?"

"This town is covered in smoke, right? So we can't see them, but above that smoke are shining stones called '*stars*.'

Not just one or two. A thousand, ten thousand, or even more."

"That's pretty dumb. You're lying, right?"

". . . My dad saw those '*stars*.' When he was far out on the ocean. At one point the smoke overhead all went away, and there were thousands of shining '*stars*' floating in the air.

Nobody in town believed him, and Dad died being called liar.

But Dad said 'There are stars above the smoke,' and told me how I could see the stars."

Lubicchi said as he looked up at the smoke.

"'Believe. Even if you're the only one.'"

幻 夢

第二天，普佩尔来到约好的地方，身上又散发出臭味。

第三天，第四天，接下来的每一天都是如此。

“普佩尔，你天天洗澡，怎么还是那么臭呀。”

卢比奇捏着鼻子说，但还是坚持每天给普佩尔洗澡。

Next day, when Poupelle came to the meeting place, his body was letting out the stench again.
And the next day, and the next day, too.
“Poupelle, your body gets smelly no matter how much we wash it.”
Lubicchi pinched his nose and muttered how smelly it was, but he washed Poupelle’s body every day.

这一天，普佩尔看上去和平常不太一样。

“怎么啦？发生什么事了？”

原来，普佩尔的左耳朵掉了。

“他们说，我把城里搞得又脏又乱。”

“你的耳朵还能听到吗？”

“听不到，什么也听不到了。耳朵掉了，就听不到声音了。”

“肯定是安东尼奥他们干的，真是太过分了！”

“谁让我是个怪物呢，没办法。”

One day.
Poupelle showed up looking very different.
“What's wrong, Poupelle? What in the world happened?”
The trash on Poupelle's left ear had fallen off.
“They say I'm littering the town.”
“Can you hear?”
“No, I can't hear anything in my left ear. I guess when the trash on my left ear falls off, I lose hearing in my left ear.”
“Antonio and his gang did this, didn't they? How terrible.”
“They can't help it. I'm a monster.”

青春組立式キット
ひるぜん
悠悠
金物店
市毛建材
ハニー美容室
火の用心
28
39

第二天，卢比奇被安东尼奥和其他几个孩子围住了。

“喂，卢比奇，丹尼斯感冒了，肯定是垃圾人传染的。”

“普佩尔每天都洗澡，根本没有什么病菌！”

“你撒谎！垃圾人昨天还臭气熏天的。你和你爸爸一样，都是大骗子！”

不过，正像他们说的那样，无论怎么洗，普佩尔还是臭臭的。卢比奇无法反驳。

“你为什么非要跟垃圾人在一起？聪明点儿的话，就应该跟我们一起玩儿！”

The next day, Lubicchi was surrounded by Antonio and his gang.
“Hey, Lubicchi. Dennis is sick with a cold.
He probably got germs from the trashman.”
“Poupelle washes his body. He doesn't have germs!”
“What a big fat liar! That trashman was stinky yesterday, too.
Your family are all liars.”
Indeed, regardless of how much they washed, Poupelle's body became smelly by the following morning.
Lubicchi had nothing to say back.
“Why do you play with that trashman, anyway. Read between the lines. You should be with us.”

ヒミツ市

卢比奇垂头丧气地走在回家的路上，普佩尔跟了上来。

“喂，卢比奇，我们去玩儿吧！”

“你怎么又变臭啦！都是因为你，我今天在学校被人欺负，

都是因为你身上洗不掉的臭味！”

“对不起，卢比奇。”

“我再也不想见到你了，也不想和你一起玩儿了。”

As Lubicchi was plodding home, Poupelle showed up.
“Hey Lubicchi. Let’s go play.”
“. . . You’re smelly again. I got bullied at school today because of that.
Because of your body that’s stinky no matter how much we wash it!”
“I’m sorry, Lubicchi.”
“I can’t see you anymore. I’m not playing with you anymore.”

幻 夢

那天以后，普佩尔和卢比奇就不再见面了。

和卢比奇分开后，普佩尔就没有洗过澡。苍蝇成群地围着他飞，

他变得越来越脏，越来越臭。

普佩尔的名声也越来越臭，没有人愿意接近他。

The two of them stopped seeing each other after that.

After he stopped playing with Lubicchi, Poupelle stopped washing his body, so he got even dirtier.

Flies swarmed around him, and he became filthier and filthier, smellier and smellier.

Poupelle's reputation kept getting worse.

Nobody came near Poupelle anymore.

グッドコマーシャル
朝丘真理
嶋内友和
柳生一江
鈴木美奈子
KEEP OUT
MOTHER WARS
丸橋優菜
マキノ優
Yoke
桝田泰司

一个寂静的夜晚，有人在敲卢比奇的窗户。

卢比奇向窗外一看，是普佩尔！面目全非的普佩尔！

他浑身黑漆漆的，看上去肮脏不堪，还少了一只胳膊。

肯定又被安东尼奥他们欺负了。卢比奇赶紧打开了窗户。

“怎么啦，普佩尔，不是说好不再见面了……”

“走，跟我走！”

“你说什么？”

“快跟我走啊，卢比奇！”

One quiet night.
There was a knock on Lubicchi's window.
When Lubicchi looked toward the window, Poupelle was there, barely recognizable.
His body was black with grime, and he was missing an arm.
It must have been Antonio and the gang must have done it again.
Lubicchi quickly opened the window.
"What's wrong, Poupelle? We're not supposed to . . . "
". . . Let's go."
"What are you saying?"
"Let's go, Lubicchi."

“等一下，到底发生什么事啦？”

“来不及了，快一点，在我生命结束之前一起去！”

“去哪儿呀？”

“快跟我走，来不及了，来不及了！”

“Wait a second. What in the world is wrong?”

“We gotta hurry. Let's go before they take my life away.”

“Where're we going?”

“We have to hurry. We gotta hurry.”

他们来到一片无人光顾的海滩。

“上船，卢比奇，快上船！”

“你要干嘛？这条船坏了，没法开了啊。”

普佩尔并不在意，他从口袋里掏出很多气球，

啊噗——啊噗——，他使劲吹气球。

啊——噗——噗——，啊——噗——噗——。

“喂，普佩尔，你这是要干嘛？”

啊——噗——噗——，啊——噗——噗——。

“来不及了，来不及了，在我生命结束之前一起去！”

普佩尔把吹好的气球一个接一个拴到船上。

They got to a sandy beach where nobody visits.
"Let's go, Lubicchi. Hop on."
"What are you talking about? This ship is broken, it's not going anywhere."
Poupelle didn't care, and pulled out a whole bunch of balloons from his pocket.
He huffed and puffed and blew up the balloons.
Huff puff, huff puff.
"Hey Poupelle, what're you doing?"
Huff puff, huff puff.
"We gotta hurry. We need to hurry. Before they take my life away."
Then, Poupelle tied the inflated balloons to the ship, one by one.

那艘船被几百只气球吊了起来。

“快上来，卢比奇。”

“去哪儿？”

“烟雾上面，”普佩尔解开船的缆绳，

“我们去看星星！”

Hundreds of balloons were tied to the ship.

"Let's go, Lubicchi."

"Where . . . ?"

"Above the smoke."

Poupelle said as he untied the rope anchoring the ship.

"Let's go see the stars."

气球吊着船，缓缓地升上了天空。

“这样能行吗？！”

这是卢比奇第一次从这么高的地方俯瞰全城，

烟囱之城的夜景很美。

“屏住呼吸，马上要进入烟雾层了。”

The ship with the balloons lifted off the ground and slowly floated in mid-air.
"Are you sure this is OK??"
It was the first time Lubicchi saw the town from this height.
The night view of the town was beautiful.
"OK, hold your breath. We're about to go in the smoke."

呼——呼——呼——，呼——呼——呼——。

烟雾之中，到处都是漆黑一片，什么也看不见。

呼呼作响的风中传来了普佩尔的声音。

“抓紧点儿，卢比奇！”

随着他们逐渐升高，风也越来越大。

Rumble rumble rumble.
They couldn't see anything inside the smoke. It was pitch black.
Poupelle's voice could be heard between the rumbling of the wind.
"Hold tight, Lubicchi."
The wind kept getting stronger as they rose higher.

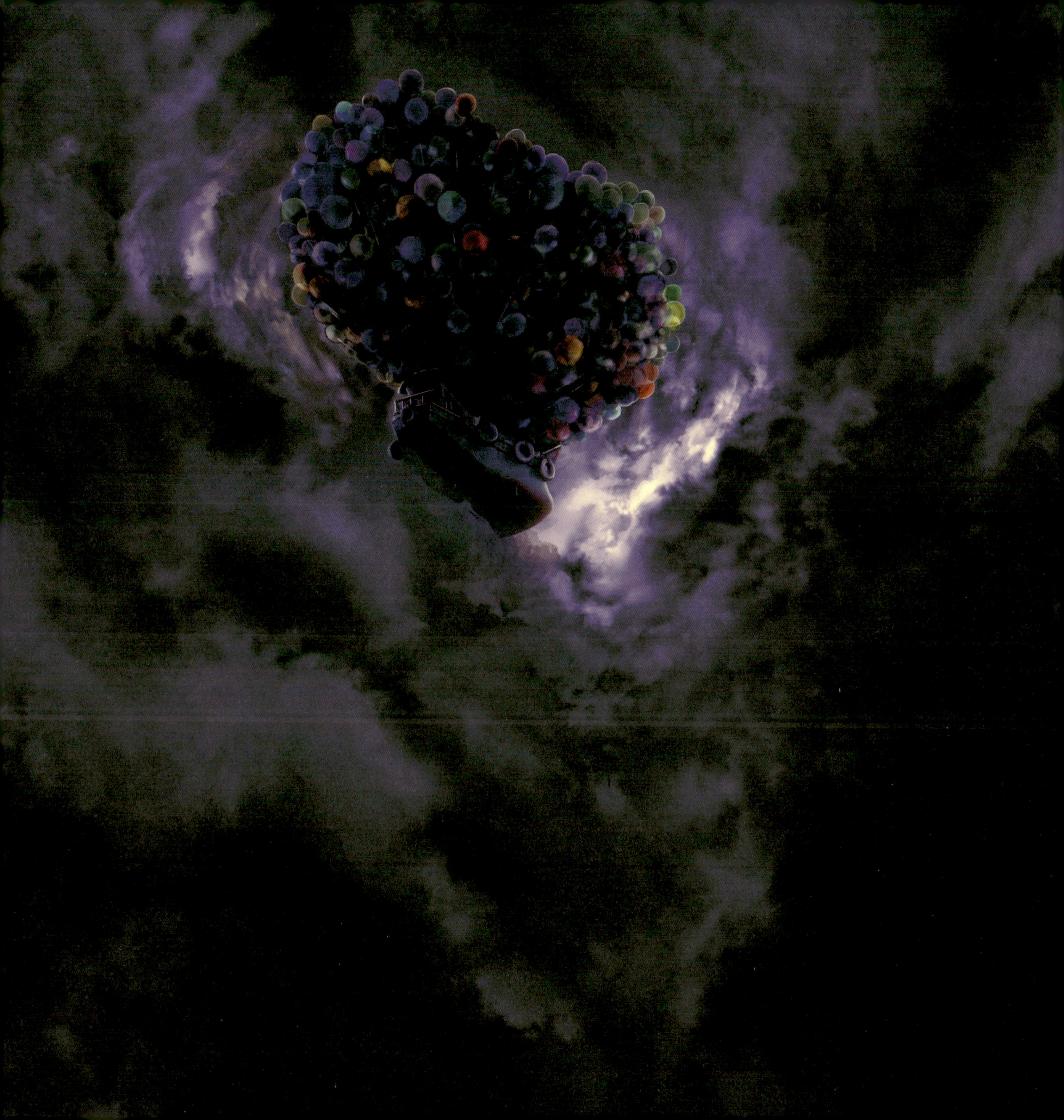

“卢比奇，向上看，我们要穿过烟雾层了！千万别闭眼啊！”

呼——呼——呼，呼——呼——呼。

“Lubicchi, look up. We’re coming out of the smoke! Don’t close your eyes.”

Rumble rumble rumble.

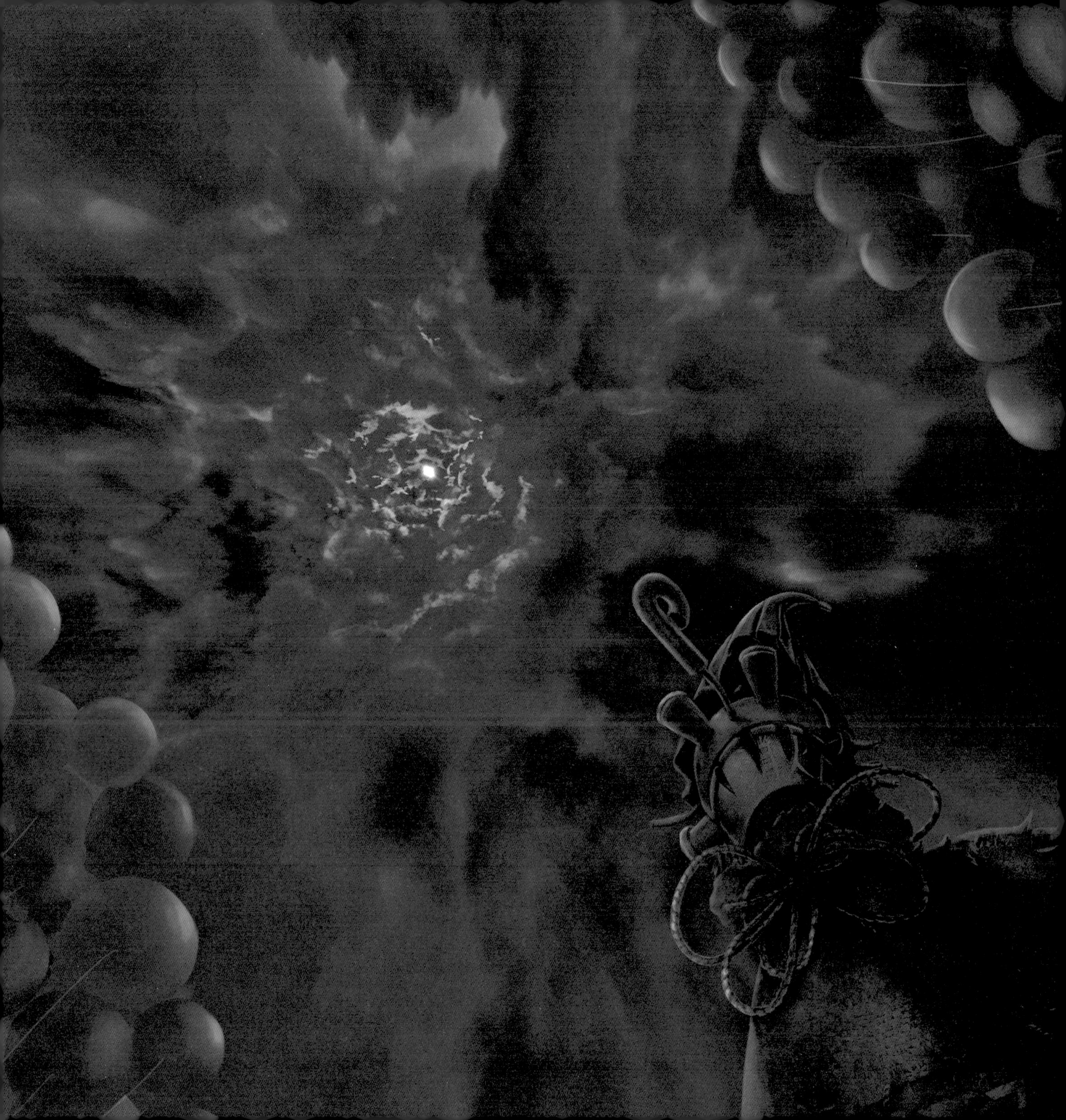

“……我爸爸没有撒谎！”

天空中布满了闪闪发光的星星，数都数不清。

过了一会儿，普佩尔静静地说：

“你回去的时候，把船上的气球解开就可以了，但是，千万不能一下子都解开，

那样船会掉下去的，你得一个接一个……”

“你说什么，普佩尔，我们不是一起回去吗？”

“在这里告别吧。能和你一起看星星，我已经非常开心了。”

“Dad wasn't lying.”

The place was filled with countless points of light.

After staring at the light for a while, Poupelle said quietly.

“When you go back, all you need to do is take the balloons off the ship, but you can't take them all off at once.

If you take them off at once, the ship is gonna fall, so one by one, one by one. . .”

“What're you talking about, Poupelle? We're going back together, right?”

“This is as far as I can go with you.

I'm really happy I got to see the '*stars*' with you.”

“你胡说什么，我们要一起回去！”

“对了，卢比奇，我一直在寻找你丢失的吊坠。

那条污水河的垃圾都被送进了垃圾处理厂，所以我猜，吊坠一定就在那里。”

“What do you mean? Let’s go back together.”
“You know, Lubicchi. I’ve been looking for that pendant you lost.
The trash in that sewage canal ends up at the waste treatment plant,
so I thought it would be there.”

“我是出生在垃圾山的垃圾人，早就习惯了掏垃圾的活儿。

我们分开后，我每天都去垃圾堆里找吊坠……

我以为，十天的时间，怎么也该找到了……”

“I'm a trashman, born in a trash pile, so I'm used to rummaging through trash.
I looked for it in the trash every day since then, but I just couldn't find it . . .
I thought it would take only ten days or so to find it . . .”

“普佩尔，所以，你的身体才……对不起！”

“没关系，你第一次和我说话时，

我就决定，不管今后发生什么，我们都是永远的朋友。”

卢比奇的眼泪流了下来。

“我没有在垃圾处理厂找到吊坠。我真是太笨了，

你以前说我身上有你‘熟悉的味道’时，我就应该想到。”

普佩尔打开头顶摇摇欲坠的破伞，

“它一直都在这里。”

“That is why your body was . . . Poupelle, I was so mean to you.”

“It doesn't matter. When you first talked to me,

I decided I'd always be your friend, no matter what.”

Tears spilled out from Lubicchi's eyes.

“And anyway, the pendant wasn't at the waste treatment plant.

I was stupid.

I should've realized it when you said ‘*You smell familiar*.’”

Poupelle opened the rickety umbrella, which was his head.

“It was here all along.”

伞内挂着一个银色的吊坠。

“你要找的东西就在这里，它是我身体的一部分。难怪你说能闻到一种熟悉的味道呢。

左耳朵掉下来后，我听不到声音了。

同样，没有这个吊坠，我就走不动了。

但它是属于你的。和你在一起，我度过了最快乐的时光。

谢谢你，卢比奇，再见……”

说着，普佩尔就要解下吊坠。

A silver pendant hung inside the umbrella.
“The pendant you've been looking for was right here. It's my brain.
This is what smelled familiar.
When the trash on my left ear fell off, I couldn't hear in my left ear anymore.
In the same way, if I lose this pendant, I'll stop moving.
But this pendant is yours. The time I spent with you,
I was truly happy. Thank you Lubicchi, goodbye . . .”
With that, Poupelle raised his hand to pull off the pendant, but then . . .

“不要！”卢比奇紧紧地抓住了普佩尔的手。

“你要干什么，卢比奇，这是属于你的吊坠呀！

我留着它，万一被安东尼奥他们抢走，就真的找不回来了。

你就永远见不到爸爸的照片了。”

“我们一起逃跑吧！”

“不行，要是他们发现你和我在一起，你会挨打的。”

“我不在乎，我们可以分担痛苦。我们再也不分开了。”

“No!”
Lubicchi grabbed Poupelle's hand.
“What're you doing, Lubicchi? This pendant is yours.
Even if I kept it, Antonio and the gang are gonna rip it off one day,
and then it will be really lost.
Then you'll never be able to see your dad's picture.”
“We can run away together.”
“Don't be silly. If you're seen with me,
they might hit you next.”
“I don't care. We can share the pain. We have each other.”

“只要有你在，我就能看到爸爸的照片。

所以，我们要天天见面，就像从前一样。”

垃圾人的眼里，滚落出大大的泪珠，

每天和卢比奇在一起……

好像是他很久很久以前就一直期待的事，那种感觉真好。

“普佩尔，星星真漂亮，谢谢你带我来。遇见你，真好！”

普佩尔有些害羞。

“Let's meet every day, Poupelle. Then, I can see Dad's picture every day.
So let's meet every day. Let's play every day, like we used to.”
Tears poured out of trashman's eyes.
Play with Lubicchi every day . . . it was a strange feeling, like something he'd been yearning for for a very long time.
“Poupelle, the stars are so beautiful. Thanks for bringing me.
I'm really happy I met you.”
Poupelle blushed and said,

“别这么说，卢比奇，我都不好意思啦。”

说着，普佩尔用食指蹭了蹭鼻子下面。

“Stop it, Lubicchi. You're embarrassing me.”

And then, he rubbed under his nose with his forefinger.

"……对不起，普佩尔，我太傻了，原来……

对呀，万圣节是逝者的灵魂回家的日子啊。"

"卢比奇，你说什么？"

"万圣节· 普佩尔，我知道你是谁了！"

". . . Poupelle. It took me a while to figure it out, too. Of course . . . of course!

Halloween is the day when the spirits of the dead come back."

"What're you talking about? Lubicchi."

"Halloween Poupelle, I know who you are now."

“谢谢你回来看我，爸爸！”

“You came to see me, Dad.”

THE END

Poupelle
INCE
Crowd Works
6%
AINT-P
ONE-COAT
EMI GLOS

职员表 Staff

作者 · 绘者 · 导演
Illustrator, Writer, Director

西野亮广 Akihiro Nishino

首席插画师
Main illustrator

六七质 munashichi

艺术指导（MUGENUP）
Art Director (MUGENUP)

岛田彬 Akira Shimada
金田旭永 Akie Kaneda
冈本裕和 Hirokazu Okamoto
石井贵纪 Takanori Ishii
家治川真弘 Masahiro Kajikawa
秋吉美保 Miho Akiyoshi
新井佳澄 Kazumi Arai

插画师（MUGENUP）
illustrator (MUGENUP)

别府满仲 Mitsunaka Beppu
寺迫良亮 Ryousuke Terasako
羽贺步 Ayumi Haga
青木真由美 Mayumi Aoki
冈本敏郎 Toshiro Okamoto
泽野雄介 Yusuke Sawano
山本麻美 Asami Yamamoto
崛口晃世 Akiyo Horiguchi
青木大地 Daichi Aoki
刘宁飞 Liu Ningfei
上野聪子 Akiko Ueno
中野纱央里 Saori Nakano
井上崇幸 Takayuki Inoue
坪田绫子 Ayako Tsubota
濑尾友华里 Yukari Seo
景山知枝 Tomoe Kageyama
芦野优纪 Yuki Ashino
古馆幸一 Kouichi Furudate
Kyu

3D 建模（MUGENUP）
3D modeling (MUGENUP)

木下洋辅 Yosuke Kinoshita

插画师 Illustrator

濑尾辰也 Tatsuya Seo
Studio Suuuu Studio Suuuu
嘉志高久 Takahisa Kashi

助理制作（MUGENUP）
Production assistant (MUGENUP)

所泽友大 Tomohiro Shozawa

制作统筹（MUGENUP）
Production supervisor (MUGENUP)

Antoine Perrin

LOGO 设计
Title Logo Designer

Ko Hayashi

图书设计 Book designer

名久井直子 Naoko Nakui

翻译 Translator

村田悟 Satoru Murata

图书编辑 Book editor

馆野晴彦（幻冬舍） Haruhiko Tateno (Gentosha)
袖山满一子（幻冬舍） Maiko Sodeyama (Gentosha)

印务经理 · 校对
Printing manager, Proofreader

田中淳史（幻冬舍） Atsushi Tanaka (Gentosha)
池田明子（幻冬舍） Meiko Ikeda (Gentosha)

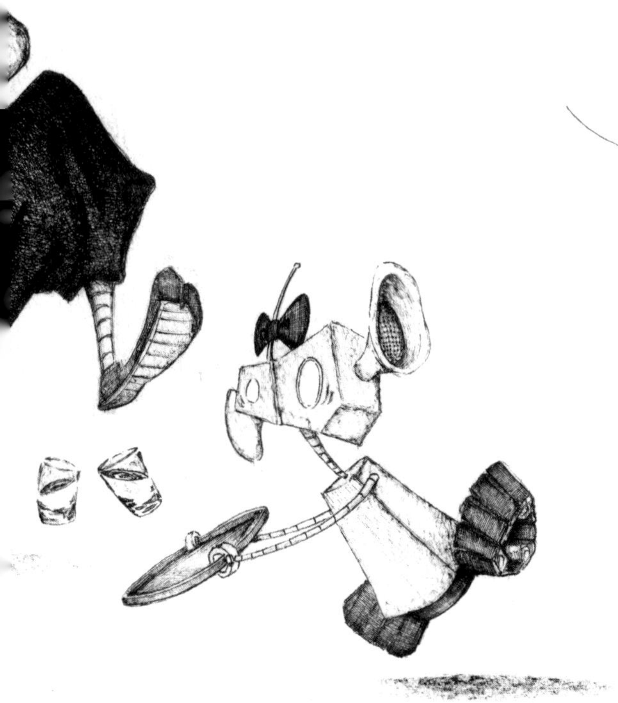

西野亮广

1980 年生于日本兵库县。

作品有《烟囱之城》《星空影院》《八音盒世界》《吉普和康提》。

曾在博客推出《西野公论》，著有小说 *Good Commercial* 等。

图书在版编目（CIP）数据

烟囱之城 /（日）西野亮广著 ；王志庚译 . -- 2 版
. -- 北京 ：新星出版社，2021.7（2022.3 重印）
ISBN 978-7-5133-4450-0
Ⅰ . ①烟… Ⅱ . ①西… ②王… Ⅲ . ①儿童故事－图
画故事－日本－现代 Ⅳ . ① I313.85
中国版本图书馆 CIP 数据核字 (2021) 第 060514 号

烟囱之城
[日] 西野亮广 著
王志庚 译

责任编辑 汪　欣
特约编辑 董碧沙
封面设计 续　超
内文制作 张　典
责任印制 李珊珊

出　　版 新星出版社　www.newstarpress.com
出 版 人 马汝军
社　　址 北京市西城区车公庄大街丙 3 号楼　邮编 100044
电话（010)88310888　传真（010)65270449
发　　行 新经典发行有限公司
电话（010)68423599　邮箱 editor@readinglife.com

印　　刷 北京奇良海德印刷股份有限公司
开　　本 889mm×1330mm　1/24
印　　张 3.75
字　　数 5千字
版　　次 2021年7月第二版　　2022年3月第三次印刷
书　　号 ISBN 978-7-5133-4450-0
定　　价 79.00元